FAKE OUT

By Rich Wallace
for younger readers:

Sports Camp

Kickers:
   #1 The Ball Hogs
   #2 Fake Out
   #3 Benched
   #4 Game-Day Jitters

KICKERS

Book 2

FAKE OUT

by **Rich Wallace**

illustrated by **Jimmy Holder**

Alfred A. Knopf

New York

Text copyright © 2010 by Rich Wallace
Illustrations copyright © 2010 by Jimmy Holder

All rights reserved. Published in the United States by Alfred A. Knopf, an imprint of
Random House Children's Books, a division of Random House, Inc., New York.

Knopf, Borzoi Books, and the colophon are registered trademarks
of Random House, Inc.

Visit us on the Web! www.randomhouse.com/kids

Educators and librarians, for a variety of teaching tools, visit us at
www.randomhouse.com/teachers

Library of Congress Cataloging-in-Publication Data
Wallace, Rich.
Kickers : fake out / Rich Wallace ; [illustrations by Jimmy Holder]. — 1st ed.
p.   cm.
Summary: Nine-year-old Ben and other members of the Bobcats co-ed soccer team
improve their skills and begin to win, especially after Ben learns the importance of
concentration from his older brother and finally masters the fake-out.
ISBN 978-0-375-85755-3 (trade) — ISBN 978-0-375-95755-0 (lib. bdg.) —
ISBN 978-0-375-89633-0 (e-book)
[1. Soccer—Fiction. 2. Teamwork (Sports)—Fiction. 3. Determination (Personality
trait)—Fiction. 4. Behavior—Fiction. 5. Family life—Fiction.] I. Holder, Jimmy, ill.
II. Title. III. Title: Fake out.
PZ7.W15877Kif 2010
[Fic]—dc22
2009021350

The text of this book is set in 12-point Goudy.

Printed in the United States of America
August 2010
10 9 8 7 6 5 4 3 2 1
First Edition

THE BOBCATS

Team Roster

Ben

Mark

Erin

Shayna

Omar

Jordan

Darren

Kim

Coach Patty

CHAPTER ONE
Stuck in Concrete

Ben ran toward the soccer ball, eager to stop the rush of the Panthers. His team held a narrow 2–1 lead with just a few minutes remaining.

"Go, Bobcats!" yelled Ben's teammate Erin, who was on the sideline. "Get that ball."

A Panther player reached the ball first, and he sprinted down the field. The kid was taller than Ben and very thin. Ben moved into his path, ready to knock the ball free.

From the corner of his eye, Ben could see players from both teams rushing toward the goal area. It was a blur of blue shirts on the Bobcats and green ones on the Panthers.

The Panther ran along the sideline, skillfully controlling the ball. But Ben stayed with him, not allowing him to angle across toward the goal.

The player stopped suddenly, stepping on the ball and pulling it back toward him. Ben stumbled as he tried to pivot, and the Panther sent a crisp pass to a teammate.

Ben's teammate Mark cut off that player's path, and another Bobcat ran over to help out. They had him trapped!

He has to pass, Ben thought. *Get ready to spring!*

The player Ben had been covering looped behind his teammate and yelled for the ball. The pass bounced wildly toward him, but

he fielded it cleanly and came face to face with Ben.

Ben stood squarely this time, keeping himself between the ball and the goal. *He won't get around me,* Ben thought.

The Panther dribbled the ball straight at Ben, then dodged to his left. Ben sprang in that direction, but suddenly the Panther was past him, taking the ball the other way. In two quick steps, he was in front of the goal, and he fired it hard into the net.

The game was tied.

Ben couldn't believe it. He'd been faked out, and it had cost the Bobcats a goal.

"Let's move!" shouted Mark. "There's still time."

But time was running out quickly. The Bobcats moved up the field, but the Panthers were playing tight defense.

Mark passed to Ben, and Ben put his head

down and charged. A trio of players in green shirts blocked his path, so Ben turned and passed the ball to Jordan.

But no one got off another shot. The referee blew his whistle and the game ended.

Ben hung his head as he walked off the field. Erin patted his shoulder. "Hey, a tie isn't so bad," she said. "It's better than a loss."

"Not much," Ben said. Especially since it had been his fault. He was sure he'd had that player stopped, but he'd been left flat-footed as the tying goal was scored.

"That kid made you look like you were stuck in concrete," said Mark.

Ben winced. Last week, he would have been ready to fight Mark over a remark like that. They'd been enemies for the first few games before starting to play like teammates. Was Mark starting all over again with the nonsense?

Ben glared at Mark.

"It's okay," Mark said with a slight smile. "He did it to me, too."

Ben shook his head and kicked at the turf. The Bobcats' coach had taught them all about shooting and passing, but a fake like that one seemed very advanced for a league mostly full of beginners. The kids in this program were nine and ten years old.

"How did he learn a move like that?" Ben asked.

"Who knows?" Mark said. "Where's a ball?"

Ben stepped to the bench and rolled a ball out from under it with his foot. He swept it over to Mark.

"It was like this," Mark said. He stepped toward the ball and moved it with his right foot, kicking it over to the left. Then he stopped and kicked it quickly to the right. He stumbled as he kicked it again, but the ball moved in the opposite direction.

"Pretty good," Ben said. "It was something like that."

"We need to practice until we can make that move on the run," Mark said.

"Yeah, and we need to learn how to defend against it, too," Ben said. "We both got burned today. It cost us a win."

The Bobcats had lost their first two games of the Kickers League season, partly because Mark and Ben wouldn't pass to each other. They were two of the best players on the team, and they'd finally learned that it took a lot of teamwork to win a soccer game.

But Mark and Ben both had scored in the third game, finally figuring out that passing was much more effective than trying to dribble the length of the field by yourself. They'd won that game. So today's tie left their record at one win, two losses, and a tie.

The Bobcats' next several games were also against teams from the other division. Then they'd have rematches with the three teams in their own division. After that, the top two teams in each division would compete in the play-offs.

Ben glanced over at the Panthers, who were huddled up around their coach. They looked excited. And happy. Ben and his teammates weren't even smiling. They'd led for nearly the entire game, so letting a win slip away in the final seconds really hurt.

Their game had been the last one of the day, so the officials were already posting the updated standings on a bulletin board near the parking lot. Ben walked over to have a look. He saw that the Bobcats had a lot of ground to make up before they could even think about getting a play-off spot.

"Looks like we can get back on track next

week," Mark said. "The Falcons haven't won a single game."

Ben shrugged. "We've only won once," he said. "But you're right. Nobody will burn me like that again, I can promise you."

The kid who'd faked Ben out went running past, heading for the parking lot. "Nice game," he said, flashing a big grin.

"You too," Ben mumbled. He couldn't tell if the kid was rubbing it in or if he really was congratulating him. It didn't matter. The kid *had* played a nice game. Ben had just been his victim.

KICKERS

NORTHERN DIVISION

	Win	Loss	Tie
Sharks	3	1	0
Rabbits	3	1	0
Tigers	1	2	1
Bobcats	1	2	1

SOUTHERN DIVISION

	Win	Loss	Tie
Panthers	2	0	2
Eagles	1	1	2
Wolves	1	2	1
Falcons	0	3	1

Today's scores:

Eagles 1, Tigers 1

Sharks 4, Wolves 2

Rabbits 3, Falcons 1

Panthers 2, Bobcats 2

Next week:

Wolves vs. Tigers

Bobcats vs. Falcons

Rabbits vs. Panthers

Eagles vs. Sharks

CHAPTER TWO
A New Move

Ben's parents hadn't been able to make it to the game, so he and Erin had to walk home. They lived on the same block and had been friends since first grade. It wasn't a long walk, but Ben was tired from running hard for an hour.

He stopped and peeked in the window at the market. He could see a cooler of sports drinks and soda bottles.

"A cold drink would be great," Ben said. His water bottle was empty but he didn't have any money. So he'd have to wait until he got home.

"You could have some of my water," Erin said, holding out her bottle to him.

Ben winced. "No way," he said. "It looks like warm spit."

"Thanks a lot," Erin said. She looked at the bottle and frowned. There was only about an inch of water left in it. She took off the cap and drank it. Then she stuck her tongue out at Ben. "It's warm, but it's not spit."

Ben let out a sigh and wiped the sweat from his forehead. He could still see the kid making that move, sending Ben sprawling in the wrong direction as he took a direct path to the goal. Ben's heart sank again as he thought about the ball rippling into the net.

He started walking, kicking at a stone and sending it into the street.

"What are you doing after lunch?" Erin asked. "Want to come over?"

Ben stared straight ahead. "Nope."

"Why not? It's a beautiful day."

"I just don't feel like it."

"Why not?"

"Because I *don't*, that's why."

Erin shook her head. "You sure are a grouch today."

They walked two more blocks before Ben said anything. When they reached the corner by Erin's house, he said, "We shou. ve won that game."

"So? We tied."

"We should have *won*. Don't you ?"

"Yes, I care. But I'm not going to let it ruin my day." Erin turned and waved to her dad, who was trimming the edge of their lawn. "So I'll see you later. Or not," she said.

Ben walked away. How could Erin be so cheerful after a game like that?

He let the back door slam on his way into the house and kicked his shoes down the cellar stairs. He walked into the kitchen, opened the refrigerator and drank some orange juice right out of the carton.

"That's gross," said his older brother, Larry, who was thirteen. "The rest of us drink that stuff, too, you know."

Ben wiped his mouth with the sleeve of his soccer jersey. "I was thirsty," he said.

"So was I," Larry said. "Guess I'll have some water."

Ben took another swig of the juice.

"Mom!" Larry called. "Ben's drinking out of the carton again."

Their mother came into the kitchen. "Ben, I've told you not to do that."

"It's gross," Larry said.

"You already said that!" Ben set the carton on the shelf and closed the refrigerator door.

"And you got grime all over the door handle," Mom said. "Why didn't you wash your hands first?"

"Because I was dying of thirst."

"Well, get a paper towel and clean it up," Mom said. "And wash your hands."

"Don't rush me."

"What?"

"I said, I'll do it in a minute. I'm starving. I just played a soccer game, remember?"

Mom pointed toward the bathroom. "Don't mess up the towels," she said.

Ben walked to the bathroom. "I guess nobody cares if we won or not," he said loudly. He slammed the bathroom door.

When he came back to the kitchen, he said, "I need lunch."

"I need lunch, *please*," said Mom. "You're acting like a total brat today, Ben."

"Well, none of you came to my game and you didn't even ask how we did."

"We've been to every one of your games so far. Larry had a cross-country race this morning. You know that."

"And you didn't ask how *I* did either, Ben," Larry said.

"Well, *we* had a terrible game," Ben said.

"That's too bad," Mom said. "Larry ran very well."

"Big deal."

"It *is* a big deal. . . . I think you'd better go spend some time in your room until you've got a better attitude," Mom said.

"I'm starving."

"You'll live."

So Ben stomped off to his room and flopped onto the bed. Nobody seemed to get it. He'd played poorly, at least at the end of the game. Didn't he have a right to be angry?

He looked around the room. He had a giant *Tyrannosaurus rex* poster on the wall above his bed, and a Boston Bruins hockey jersey hanging on the one directly across from it. Books and toys were in fairly neat piles on the floor. He glanced around the room for his soccer ball, then remembered that it was out in the yard.

Halloween was about a month away, and his mom had put a plastic jack-o'-lantern on his dresser. It was about the same size as a soccer ball, but it had a flat bottom.

Ben took it down and laid it on its side so it would roll. He stepped back a few feet, imagining an opponent just in front of him. He brought his right foot forward and swept the pumpkin out in front of him. He leaned hard to his right, then shifted to the left and raised his right foot, bringing it over the top of the "ball" and replanting it on the other side. Then he nudged the ball with the outside of his right foot, sending it in the opposite direction.

In his mind, the opponent was left there, lunging in the wrong direction as Ben smoothly went the other way.

That's it! he thought. *That's how the guy burned me.* Ben had stepped over the ball without touching it, then swept it back with the outside of his foot.

He practiced it a few more times, trying to go faster with each attempt. Then he put the pumpkin back where it belonged and headed downstairs.

"Sorry, Mom," he said. "I was mad because I messed up the game."

"Well, maybe you'll feel better after you eat."

"I already feel better," he said. "Could I have a peanut butter sandwich?"

"Sure."

"Maybe two?"

"I don't see why not."

"Thanks. Then I'm going to practice in the yard for a while. I'm working on a new move. Wait'll you see it. It's going to be great!"

Next game, Ben thought, *I'll be the one with the fancy footwork.*

CHAPTER THREE
Slipping and Stumbling

The last day of September was crisp and cool, with red and yellow maple leaves beginning to fall from the trees. Ben grabbed for a leaf as he jogged near the edge of the soccer field, lunging for it as it swirled in the breeze. He missed it, and it settled on the lush green grass.

"Faked out again, huh?" came a familiar voice. Mark had seen the whole thing.

"By a *leaf* this time," Ben said with a laugh.

He nodded to Mark, who was the second one to arrive for practice. Ben had been the first by about fifteen minutes. He'd come directly from school, having kept his soccer shoes and his shin guards in his backpack all day because he was so eager to get to the field.

Ben wasn't sure if he liked Mark yet, but at least they'd learned to work together on the soccer field.

"Where's your girlfriend?" Mark asked.

"*Friend*," Ben replied. "Not girlfriend."

"Just kidding," Mark said.

Erin wasn't with Ben today. It was Rosh Hashanah, so her family was observing the holiday with relatives.

Ben had forgotten to bring his ball, so he'd been running laps to warm up. He had so much energy that he could run all day. But he couldn't wait to be playing soccer. Especially after what had happened in Saturday's game.

Coach Patty arrived with her daughter, Shayna, and the rest of the team soon followed. Patty blew her whistle and gathered the team around her.

"Did I miss a rainstorm?" she asked with a grin, looking at Ben. "Somebody got wet."

Ben blushed. "I've been running," he said. "Got a little sweaty."

"A little? You look like you swam across the pond."

Ben laughed and wiped his forehead. He knew the coach was kidding.

Coach opened a large mesh bag and rolled out several soccer balls. "Let's work on passing and shooting today, then we'll scrimmage for a while. Sound good?"

Ben raised his hand. "Can we work on fakes?"

"I suppose we could. Do you guys think you're ready for that?"

"The other teams sure are!" Mark said. "We got burned on Saturday."

Ben demonstrated the move he'd worked on all weekend, stepping over the ball and pushing it back with the outside of his foot. Everybody tried it a few times.

"Okay, let's do it with a defender," Coach said after everyone had successfully made the move.

They formed two lines—one to defend and the other to move the ball. Ben was first in the line that would try the fake. Shayna was set to defend.

Coach blew her whistle and Ben began dribbling up the field. Shayna crouched slightly and moved toward him at an angle, pinning Ben near the sideline.

When Shayna was about five feet away, Ben tapped the ball toward the middle of the field, then took a quick step to keep up with it. He tried to step over the ball, but it was moving faster than when he'd tried this move alone. His foot hit the top of the ball and Ben slid back. Shayna took control and dribbled quickly toward the goal.

Coach blew her whistle. "Nice try, Ben," she said. "And good defense, Shayna. It's a lot harder to make that move on the run, but let's keep working at it. Get back in line . . . who's next?"

They worked on the fake for about fifteen minutes, and most of the time it didn't work. Players slipped and tripped and the ball squirted away, but once in a while someone had success.

Ben finally made the move just right, leaving Mark behind as he raced along the sideline with the ball.

About time, Ben thought.

"Let's scrimmage!" Coach called. "Work

that fake in if you have the chance, but don't get carried away with it. Passing is still your best option. Pass the ball and run to an open spot for a return pass. That's how to move the soccer ball."

Because there were only seven players, Coach decided to create a shorter field. She set up two sets of cones about forty yards apart to use as goals.

"We'll play three against three, with one substitute," she said. "Shayna, Mark, and Omar on one side; Jordan, Kim, and Darren on the other. No goalies. Work with your teammates. Remember the triangle."

Ben gave Coach a surprised look.

"You'll play plenty," she said. "Stay warm."

Ben took a ball and dribbled along the sideline, trying to keep it close. He practiced stopping and starting, throwing little shoulder moves that would confuse an opponent.

He imagined leaving a defender behind, just as had happened to him in Saturday's game.

When he finally got onto the field, he was surprised how open it felt. With just six players out there, he had plenty of room to run. By moving together in a flexible triangle shape, he and his teammates were able to make a series of open passes.

"Kim!" he called, dropping back as his teammate got trapped near the sideline. She turned and passed the ball to Ben, and he took it on the run.

Jordan was open to Ben's left. Ben took another step with the ball as Mark and Omar darted over to defend. As they closed in, Ben passed the ball sideways to Jordan, then drifted back toward the center of the field.

As the defenders moved toward Jordan, Ben cut between them. Jordan sent the ball streaming across the grass, and Ben took it cleanly as he closed in on the goal. Only Shayna had a chance to stop him.

Ben raced toward the left side of the goal, then softly passed to Kim. She was alone in front of the cones, and she easily tapped it in for a score.

"Great teamwork!" Coach shouted. "See what happens when we pass? And when we move to get open?"

Ben bumped his fist against Kim's, then trotted back to play defense. Making a pass like that felt as good as scoring a goal.

Mark came flying down the field, straight at Ben. At the last second, he tried to make the move, stepping over the ball and knocking it back. But Ben saw it coming a mile away. He stepped in and knocked the ball loose, sending it up the line toward Kim.

Ben was several steps ahead of Mark,

and the goal was wide open in front of him. Kim sent a brisk pass toward the front of the goal, and Ben ran it down. Another easy shot and another goal. Ben's team was looking strong.

"Good *thinking*," Coach said, clapping her hands. "Sometimes your best weapon in soccer is your brain."

Ben looked at Kim and grinned. She'd been playing well lately. In fact, Ben could see a lot of improvement in all of his teammates. He was certain that they'd get a lot of wins before the season was over.

"Play-offs, here we come!" Ben called.

"Long way to go," Mark said. "But nothing we can't handle."

"Time for a switch," Coach said. She waved Darren back onto the field.

"Who's going out?" Ben asked.

"Nobody," Coach replied. "One thing to

know about soccer is that there are a lot of mis-matches. Sometimes you'll be all alone on defense with three or four opponents around you. You have to know how to react when you're outnumbered."

"So it's four-on-three?" Ben asked.

"Yes. Darren will join Mark's team. Let's see if they can slow down that awesome Ben-Kim combination."

Ben blushed a little and shook his head, but he broke into a smile. He and Kim had made a couple of great passes. It was a terrific feeling to click like that.

Mark's team managed to score, but then Jordan showed some excellent footwork to put Ben's team in position again. He passed to Ben, who faked a pass to Kim and sent it back to Jordan. By passing back and forth and moving quickly, Ben's team kept control of the ball despite being outnumbered.

Kim finally took a shot, but Omar ran it down and kicked it over to Shayna.

"Spread out!" Ben called, running back on defense.

He knew the other team would always have a player open if they played a smart game, so if Ben's team bunched up they'd definitely get burned. He stayed toward the center of the field, with Jordan taking the left side and Kim the right.

Mark passed to Shayna, who passed it to Omar, who found Mark open near the corner. Mark lofted the ball toward the front of the goal, and Darren managed to control it. He took an off-balance shot. Ben got to it first and booted it up the field.

After a few more minutes of nonstop running, Ben was exhausted. But they'd kept the game even, despite having one less player.

When Coach finally blew her whistle to

halt the scrimmage, Ben flopped onto the grass and spread out on his back.

"A little tired?" Coach asked, standing over him.

"Tired and *excited*," Ben said. "I can't wait until Saturday."

CHAPTER FOUR
Two Fakes at Once

Ben arrived at the field very early for the game on Saturday, eager to warm up and watch the first match between the Eagles and the Sharks.

He saw his friend Luis "Loop" Pineda jogging toward him. He played for the Falcons, the Bobcats' opponents today.

"Hey, Loop," Ben called.

"Watch out today," Loop said. "We're ready to roll."

Ben knew that the Falcons hadn't won a single game this season. But Loop was a good athlete, so they'd probably give the Bobcats a tough time.

"We've been close in every game," Loop said. "Just haven't had the breaks go our way."

"Don't count on getting them today," Ben said. "We were *great* in practice the other day. Passing, shooting. You should have seen us." He didn't mention the faking. It seemed like he should keep that to himself.

Loop gave a sly smile. "We had a pretty good practice, too. Things are coming together."

"We'll see," Ben said.

"Yeah, we will."

Ben's teammates began to gather a while later, and they headed to the far side of the field to work on their passing skills. Ben glanced over several times to check on the Sharks-Eagles game. He also could see the Falcons in their red shirts, warming up in the distance.

Just before game time, Coach Patty had the Bobcats huddle up. "You've been working hard, people. Let's use our heads and play smart today."

"And hard!" Ben said.

"And hard," Coach repeated. "Good sportsmanship and lots of energy."

"This is a definite victory," Ben said. "No way these guys can beat us."

"Just like in practice," Kim said. "Lots of passing."

"This is our day," Jordan said. "Our big win streak starts right here. Today."

They put their hands together in the center of the huddle and called, "One. Two. Three. Bobcats!"

Ben and Shayna started as the Bobcats' defenders, with Mark, Erin, and Omar in the front line and Jordan as goalie.

"Nothing gets past us," Ben said.

Shayna nodded. She adjusted her shin guards and hopped up and down. "These guys are fast," she warned.

"So are we. Besides, if we play the way we did in practice, the ball might not even come down this way."

But it didn't take long for Ben to be proven wrong. The Falcons made some crisp passes and moved the ball down the field. No player held the ball for more than a couple of steps, firing it to a teammate and quickly moving to an open spot.

Ben sprinted toward the player with the ball and Mark headed over, too.

No way is this guy getting past me, Ben thought.

The kid was fast, as Shayna had said, but Ben was forcing him toward the sideline. When the Falcon player stepped over the ball and dodged to the side, Ben was ready. He knew that move. He knew which way the kid was going.

Ben leaned to his left but didn't commit. As he expected, the kid went that way, and Ben was ready to knock the ball away. He lunged. And just as quickly, the kid took the ball in the opposite direction, racing past Ben and into the open field.

Ben stepped back and fell, landing on his butt. He jumped up and scrambled toward the ball, but it had already been passed. Loop was open in front of the goal, fielding the ball and shooting it into the net.

"Alex left you flat-footed," Loop said as he jogged past Ben.

Less than a minute had gone by and the

Bobcats were already behind. Ben put his hands on his hips and stared at the sky. How had that happened?

"Let's get it back!" called Mark, clapping his hands. "That was a fluke. Let's go."

Ben shook his head and returned to his

position. Loop was beaming up ahead. He'd scored the goal, but it had been set up by the kid who faked out Ben.

Ben had to admit, that had been a very tricky move.

The Falcons kept up the pressure, dominating the game for most of the first half. Ben and Shayna played tough defense and Jordan made a couple of great saves, otherwise the Falcons would have built a big lead.

As they walked off the field at halftime, the score was still only 1–0. But the Bobcats had done very little on offense.

"Rest up," Coach said. "We're still in this game. One quick goal and it'll be all even."

Ben bit down on his lip and looked around. Every time he'd had the ball, a swarm of Falcons seemed to be in his face. He'd made some good passes, but just as often he'd kicked it to the other team.

"Let's get some speed on the front line," Coach said. "Jordan, Ben, and Kim. Erin and Darren on defense. Shayna in goal. Remember—be smart. Rapid passes, then move to an open spot. These guys aren't any better than you are, they're just hustling more."

Ben looked at Mark. His face was red and he was sweating. He'd been running on offense for the entire game.

"I'm sure you'll be back on the field soon," Ben said.

"Better be," Mark said. "You need me out there."

"Wonder what got into that team, anyway?" Ben said. "They lost every game, and now they look like superstars."

"Guess it just clicked," Mark said with a shrug. "We got a lot better all of a sudden, too. At least I *thought* we had."

"We did," Ben said. "You'll see. This second half will be different."

Ben jogged onto the field and began to stretch lightly. Jordan walked over to him. He was a quiet kid but very fast.

"Watch Alex's head," Jordan said, nodding toward the Falcon player who had faked Ben out at the beginning of the game.

"What for?" Ben asked. "Does he have three ears or something?"

Jordan grinned. "When he does a fake, he always looks in the direction he intends to go. He might dodge this way"—Jordan gave a quick step to his left—"but if you watch his eyes they'll be looking the other way. And that's where he'll end up."

"Good tip," Ben said.

The referee set the ball at midfield and Jordan hustled to get in position. Ben looked up the field and caught Loop's attention.

Loop squinted and patted his chest, then pointed at Ben as if he was ready to mow him down, but he was smiling, too. Ben pointed back.

With the ball in play, Ben's focus shifted entirely to the game. A one-goal difference could be wiped out in seconds.

Jordan was moving up the side of the field with the ball, so Ben hung back slightly, with Kim on the opposite side.

As Loop and another defender moved toward Jordan, Ben shouted for the ball. Jordan turned and sent it skimming across the grass, several yards in front of Ben. He was the closest one to it.

Ben could see the play developing. Kim was sprinting to his right, and the entire field was open in front of her. Ben reached the ball and didn't break stride. He dribbled once, then sent it toward Kim.

Loop and the others raced to slow Kim down, but she was nearing the goal. Still on the run, Ben looked for Jordan. They both needed to set up by the goal for a pass or a rebound.

Kim was too far to the side to shoot, but she floated a nice pass toward the front of the goal.

Ben got his foot on it, but too many Falcons were between him and the net. He knocked it awkwardly toward Jordan, who stopped it with his foot, stepped back, and fired.

The Falcons' goalie got both hands on the ball but couldn't quite grab it. It rolled to the side of the field and Loop gave it a hard boot, sending it well past midfield.

"So close," Ben called as he and Kim and Jordan ran down the field.

"Good passing!" Jordan said. "Keep up the pressure."

Soon the Bobcats made another charge at

the goal. Kim took a shot that bounced off the goalpost, and Ben lined the rebound directly into the goalie's hands. They hadn't scored, but they were dominating the second half.

Ben had the ball near midfield, moving quickly. Loop and another Falcon were blocking his path, so he pivoted and passed the ball backward toward Erin, who was following about ten yards behind.

But Ben's pass was off the mark. Alex took control of the ball and began dribbling swiftly toward the Bobcats' goal. Loop and another teammate were already moving in that direction, and they were several steps ahead of Ben. So only Darren and Shayna were between the three Falcons and the goal. A couple of nice passes set up an easy shot for Alex, and suddenly the Falcons were two goals ahead.

Ben felt as if he'd been punched in the

stomach. He shook his head and stared at the goal. The Bobcats had been playing so well—passing, dribbling, nearly scoring—but just like that it had fallen apart because he'd made a bad pass.

The Falcons didn't seem like a team that hadn't won a game all season. Today, at least, they were the best team the Bobcats had played.

It was hard to find a spark after that. Mark came onto the field and the Bobcats made a few more runs at the goal, but they couldn't manage to score.

Late in the game, Alex booted in another goal for the Falcons, and it ended 3–0.

"We're the worst," Ben said as he and Erin walked off the field. His eyes were stinging and his throat felt tight. He sniffed hard.

"Those guys were *good*," Erin said.

"And what does that say about us?" Ben

took a seat on the grass and yanked off his shin guards. "Not much."

He lay back on the grass, not wanting to move. The sky was clear and the air was warm, but Ben was steaming mad. He shut his eyes and frowned.

A few seconds passed, then he felt a nudge on his shoulder. He opened his eyes and saw Loop standing over him, smiling broadly.

"Great game," Loop said.

Ben pushed up on his elbows and looked away. "You guys got the breaks today."

"We *made* those breaks," Loop said. "About time, too. I told you we'd been playing well."

"I know," Ben said. He swatted at the air with his fist. "I said the same thing about us. *That* sure wasn't true."

"Whatever," Loop said, jogging away. "You got burnt today. See you in school."

Loop stopped a few yards away. "Hey!" he called.

Ben turned his head to look. Loop gave that same squint he'd done at halftime, patting his chest and pointing at Ben. Then he smiled and ran.

"What a jerk," Ben said.

"Chill out," Erin said. "We *did* do well. Two or three plays made all the difference in the game. Otherwise we were as good as they were."

"If we were as good as they were, we would have scored," Ben said. "Good teams get it done. We didn't. They made us look like chumps."

KICKERS

NORTHERN DIVISION

	Win	Loss	Tie
Rabbits	4	1	0
Sharks	3	2	0
Tigers	2	2	1
Bobcats	1	3	1

Today's scores:

Eagles 3, Sharks 1

Rabbits 4, Panthers 3

Falcons 3, Bobcats 0

Tigers 2, Wolves 1

SOUTHERN DIVISION

	Win	Loss	Tie
Panthers	2	1	2
Eagles	2	1	2
Wolves	1	3	1
Falcons	1	3	1

Next week:

Falcons vs. Sharks

Bobcats vs. Eagles

Rabbits vs. Wolves

Tigers vs. Panthers

CHAPTER FIVE
A Brain Sprain

Ben moped around the house all afternoon after the game.

"It's a nice day," said Mom. "Don't waste it. You should be outside."

But Ben just sat in his room, angry about losing again.

"We could play catch in the yard," Dad said a while later.

"No thanks," Ben said. He shut his door and lay on his bed, staring at the ceiling.

"Hey, knucklehead. Want to play a video game with me?" said Larry an hour later, knocking on the door.

"No."

"Are you sure?"

"I'm sure."

"Suit yourself," Larry said. But he opened the door.

"What?" Ben asked.

"It was only a soccer game," Larry said. "There'll be plenty more of them."

Ben shrugged. "Maybe not. I was so awful today they'll probably kick me out of the league."

"No, they won't."

"They should. We got pounded by the worst team in the league."

"So what?" Larry sat on the edge of the bed. "Everybody has an off day. And you know what? Everybody has great days, too."

"I sure haven't lately."

"You will. Last season my cross-country team got clobbered in a race by Arlington. But two weeks later we beat them in the league championship race."

"We won't be playing in any championship unless we get a *lot* better," Ben said.

At dinner, Mom told Ben to eat his carrots.

"I already ate some," he said.

"Eat them all."

Ben just looked at his plate. The carrots were overcooked and mushy.

"Soccer is supposed to be fun," Mom said. "Win or lose. You can't be a pain at home every time you lose a game. That's not fair to anybody."

Ben jabbed a fork into a carrot. "Losing is terrible," he said. "Especially when it was my fault."

"The whole team wins or loses," Dad said. "Not one player."

Ben frowned.

"Did you learn anything in the game?" Mom asked.

"I learned how much I hate to lose."

"But did you learn anything that can help you *win?*"

Ben thought about that for a minute. "I thought I learned that in the last game," he said. "When I got faked out. I spent the whole week working on fakes of my own. But those guys today had even better fakes. They made me look dumb."

Ben looked across at Larry. Larry had never been very good at sports, but he'd played basketball and Little League baseball. He'd joined the cross-country team when he'd entered junior high school. He'd trained hard all summer, so he'd become very fast. This was his second season in the sport.

"Hard work pays off," Larry said. "You'll see when you come to my race next weekend."

"I worked hard for a whole week," Ben said.

Larry laughed. "Sometimes it takes years."

"The season is half over!" Ben yelled.

"Lower your voice," Mom said. "You have to learn to take losing in stride, Ben."

Ben slammed his fork down. "Losing stinks."

Dad stood up. "Go to your room, Ben. If soccer is this much of a problem for you, then maybe you'd better stop playing."

"I don't want to quit."

"Then stop being a brat about it," Dad said. "Get upstairs and think this over."

Ben wiped his mouth with a napkin and got out of his seat. "I'm sorry," he said. He glanced at his plate again; he'd eaten everything except the carrots. He turned and went up to his room.

He felt better on Sunday and practiced dribbling and faking in the yard. Then he walked over to Erin's house. She'd taught him how to play chess recently. He'd never beaten her, but lately the games had been lasting longer.

"Tough game yesterday, huh?" she said as they set up the chessboard.

Ben let out his breath hard. "It sure was. It was embarrassing."

"We played well," she said. "I had fun anyway."

Ben nodded slowly. "Most of it was fun," he admitted. "I just wish we had another game today instead of having to wait until next weekend. I'd like to wipe that game right out of my mind. Instead, I'll be thinking about it all week."

"Don't think too hard," Erin said with a smile. "You'll sprain your brain."

Ben moved one of his chess pieces forward. "What I'm really not looking forward

to is seeing Loop tomorrow at school. He'll
be rubbing it in about the game for sure."

"Let him talk," Erin said, making a move
of her own. "Besides, he did play a great
game."

They made a few more moves before Ben
responded. "Loop's a good athlete, but he has a
big ego, too."

Erin laughed gently. "Just like somebody else I know."

"Who? Me?"

She nodded. Then she picked up her knight and brought it into the square where Ben's bishop was sitting. She tipped the bishop over and picked it up.

"Never saw that coming," Ben said quietly, shaking his head.

Erin sat back in her chair. She tapped the side of her head. "*Now's* the time to think," she said. "It never hurts in chess."

Ben bit down on his lip. "I'll try to remember that," he said. "But it isn't easy."

"So when Loop starts teasing you on the playground, just be patient," Erin said. "Maybe he's the bishop for now. But we've got some pretty good horses on our team. We might get another shot at him in the play-offs."

Ben nodded. The Bobcats were a long way from making the play-offs. But there was still time. They would start climbing back into the race if they could just win a few more games.

CHAPTER SIX
Duking and Juking

Monday at recess, Ben walked over to the swings and took a seat. He slowly pumped his legs and began to glide back and forth.

He looked over and saw the players in his four-square group starting their regular game. Ben played every day, but today he wasn't in the mood. Loop was in the group, and he didn't feel like talking to him. But Loop was staring at him. He caught Ben's eye and smiled. Ben looked away with a frown.

All of the fourth graders had recess at the same time, so most of Ben's soccer teammates were out on the playground, too. Mark and Erin were playing four square, and Shayna and Kim were jumping rope on the basketball court. Omar and Darren were with a group shooting baskets at the other end of the court.

"I bet I can swing higher."

Ben looked over and saw Jordan walking toward him, pointing at the swing next to Ben. He grinned and sat down.

Ben hadn't known Jordan before the soccer season, and they'd hardly spoken. But they'd made some good passes to each other lately in practice and in the games. They were both quick and played hard.

"Why no four square today?" Jordan asked.

Ben shrugged. He pumped his legs harder. "Just didn't feel like it."

"I know what you mean," Jordan said. "Still thinking about Saturday's game?"

"Yeah."

"Me too." Jordan stopped swinging and braked with both feet. "All weekend, I kept thinking about how we got burned. I was *so* sure we would beat those guys."

"So was I."

"It's like we're right on the edge of being good," Jordan said. "You know what I mean?

Just one or two steps forward and we'll be as good as anyone in the league."

"We seemed about a thousand steps behind on Saturday," Ben said.

"Yeah, but we weren't. Just a couple of plays could have made all the difference."

"That's what Erin said. But I played pretty badly."

"No, you didn't. Erin's right."

Ben stopped swinging, too. He looked around the playground. "Seen any soccer balls?"

"No, but I was thinking of bringing one tomorrow," Jordan said. "Get in some extra passing. Sound good?"

"Sounds like a plan," Ben replied. "Maybe we'll spend half of recess kicking the ball around, then switch over to four square."

Jordan jutted his chin toward Loop's group. "Speaking of four square, they could use a few players."

Ben stepped off the swing. "Let's go."

They walked across the playground and stood next to Mark, who was waiting to get back into the game. Loop and three others were smacking a pink rubber ball back and forth, trying to hold their positions in the square. After each round, one player had to leave the square and a new player would take his place.

"Look who's back," Loop said as the point ended, nodding toward Ben, then Jordan. "Ready to join the elite, huh?"

"Ready and able," Jordan said.

Loop smiled broadly. "Just watch how the pros do it," he said, serving the ball toward Mark. He kept his eyes on the game, shifting back and forth and skillfully returning the ball, but he kept chattering, too.

"See, the best players are always in motion," Loop said, swatting at the ball. He kept his hands up and shifted from foot to foot. "Duking, juking . . . it's all about speed and positioning." He took his eye off the ball for a split second, glancing at Ben. "Leaving your opponent *flat-footed*."

Ben blushed. But in that split second Mark lined the ball hard into Loop's square. It took a sharp bounce and Loop had no chance to reach it.

Ben clapped his hands. "Great demonstration," he said. "I see *exactly* what you mean. Flat-footed and burnt."

Loop scowled. He put his hands in his pockets and stepped out of the square. The other players shifted to new spots and Ben stepped in to take Loop's place.

Ben and Loop were friends, but they were rivals when it came to sports and games. Ben knew that Loop had the upper hand now, after his team had clobbered the Bobcats in soccer.

As they headed back toward class a few minutes later, Loop walked next to Ben. "So, who do you guys play this weekend?" he asked.

"The Eagles," Ben said. "I don't know much about them."

"They beat us the first week of the season," Loop said. "But that was when nobody on my team knew what we were doing. We just ran around the field like turkeys or something."

"Who do you play?" Ben asked.

"The Sharks," Loop replied. "What do you know about them?"

"We beat 'em a few weeks back," Ben said.

"Then we should bash them," Loop said. "Just like we did to you."

Ben gave Loop a light shove. "You got a lot of breaks."

"Like I said, we *made* our breaks." He shoved Ben back, but he didn't seem angry. "As far as I can tell, there isn't any team better than we are anymore. And we'll prove that over the next few weeks."

Ben just looked away. He and his teammates had to prove that they could succeed, too. Mostly they had to prove it to themselves.

CHAPTER SEVEN
Another Stumble

Ben hit the ground hard, but he rolled and stood up. He ran toward the ball, wiping his hands on his blue game shirt.

The weather had turned much cooler, and the field was damp from an overnight rain. Still, Ben was sweating and panting hard.

The Eagles had the ball and they were in a frenzy. Mark had scored an early goal for the

Bobcats, but neither team had managed to score since then.

Not much time was left in the game, so all of the black-shirted Eagles except the goalie were at the Bobcats' end of the field, frantic to tie the score.

"Defense!" Ben shouted. "Let's hang on."

One of the Eagles had the ball in the corner, and three of his teammates were near the goal, shouting for a pass. Ben moved into the goal area, too, as Mark and Jordan raced toward the ball.

Ben took a quick glance toward Erin, who was playing goalie for the Bobcats. She'd made four good saves since halftime.

Here came the ball, soaring through the air on a path that would put it directly in front of the goal. Ben firmed up his stance, bracing to jump. There were Eagles on both sides of him, ready to do the same.

Ben got there first. He brought his head back slightly, then poked it forward, meeting the ball with his forehead and knocking it away from the goal.

That worked, Ben thought, a bit surprised. He'd seen older players "head" the ball, but he'd never tried it in a game.

The ball drifted to the side, and Mark reached it. He turned toward the goal, then spun and dribbled quickly toward the sideline. Ben angled over and shouted, "Here!"

It would be a dangerous pass, but Mark had no choice. Two Eagles players were blocking his path, so he passed back to Ben. Ben took control and sliced past two more opponents. He had a clear field ahead.

The gap closed quickly, but Ben had time to send a crisp pass over to Jordan, who was running in the same direction. Mark made a smart move and circled behind Jordan, and the three Bobcats sprinted up the field toward the Eagles' goal.

A series of sharp passes kept the ball moving upfield. First Jordan, then Ben, and then Mark dribbled and passed.

As they reached the goal area, Ben had the ball, with one defender at his side.

Do that fake, he told himself.

Step over the ball!

Ben dodged to his right, then stepped over the ball and brought it back to his left.

Now run with it.

The move almost worked, but Ben slipped on the wet grass and the defender knocked the ball away.

I stink at this!

The ball flew on a line drive, right at Jordan's chest. But Jordan leaned back and let the ball roll off his chest to the ground. He was in perfect position for a shot, and he drove the ball into the goal.

Ben felt a huge rush of energy as he watched the ball whoosh into the net. Jordan had given the Bobcats a 2–0 lead.

"Awesome!" Jordan shouted.

Ben looked at his parents, who were on the sideline clapping. He raised his fist. But he was embarrassed about tripping over the ball.

"Everybody get back!" Mark called. "Tough defense now! Don't let up for a second."

Even the Eagles' goalie came down on offense now, but the Bobcats were ready. Any time the Eagles made a charge, either Ben or Jordan or Shayna seemed to be there to stop it.

Erin had to make one more save, but it was on a soft shot from a long distance away. She caught it easily and punted it far up the field.

The whistle blew soon after, and the Bobcats had their second win of the season.

Ben smacked hands with Jordan and ran off the field. The Bobcats gathered around Coach Patty. Everybody was jumping and shouting, but Ben couldn't help but feel that he almost cost his team the victory.

The Eagles could have scored when Ben lost the ball. He was lucky Jordan had stepped up.

"Great effort," Coach said. "That's what I like to see."

"We were rolling," said Kim. "This was our day."

They all put their hands into the center of the circle and yelled, "Bobcats!"

Ben scooped up his sweatshirt and joined Erin and Jordan as they walked toward the bleachers.

"Great recovery after I messed up that fake," Ben said.

"You *almost* made it," Jordan said.

"I know. I don't know what happened. I thought through every part of the fake, but then I messed it up at the end."

Jordan grinned. "Don't think so hard," he said. "Just let it happen."

"That's easy for you to say."

Jordan laughed. "Sooner or later it'll be natural for us. Thinking about it just leads to trouble."

Loop and Alex from the Falcons were standing nearby. Their legs were covered with mud from the field. They'd played the game before Ben's and had routed another opponent.

"You guys looked pretty good," Alex said as Ben walked past.

"*Pretty* good is right," Loop said. "Better than last week, that's for sure."

Ben stopped. He gave Loop a hard look, but Loop was smiling and didn't sound too smug.

"Not bad for a couple of last-place teams," Ben said. He wanted to remind Alex and Loop that both of their teams still had a long way to go, but he didn't want to be mean either. The two teams had the exact same records.

"I don't know about you guys, but we aren't in last place anymore," Loop said. "Things are getting much tighter in this league. It's still anybody's championship to win."

And it could be ours, Ben thought.

All of that hard work was certainly paying off now. He knew he'd played the best game of his life except for that stumble. Every member of the Bobcats had improved so much since the start of the season.

Ben pulled his sweatshirt on over his head. He stood with Alex, Loop, and Erin and watched the next two teams warming up on the field. He knew that the Rabbits had the best record in the league, but he wanted to get a look at the Wolves. They were the Bobcats' next opponent.

Ben heard his father calling from the parking lot. "Time to go!" he yelled.

"I'll see you guys at school," Ben said. "And who knows? We might get another shot at your team in the play-offs."

Loop turned to Ben. "That would be fine by me," he said. "But there's a long way to go before anybody should be thinking about the play-offs. Or a championship."

"Guess you're right," Ben said. But after the Bobcats had played so well today, he could allow himself to think about it a little.

KICKERS

NORTHERN DIVISION

	Win	Loss	Tie
Rabbits	5	1	0
Sharks	3	3	0
Tigers	2	3	1
Bobcats	2	3	1

SOUTHERN DIVISION

	Win	Loss	Tie
Panthers	3	1	2
Eagles	2	2	2
Falcons	2	3	1
Wolves	1	4	1

Today's scores:

Falcons 4, Sharks 1

Bobcats 2, Eagles 0

Rabbits 4, Wolves 2

Panthers 3, Tigers 2

Next week:

Rabbits vs. Eagles

Panthers vs. Sharks

Bobcats vs. Wolves

Tigers vs. Falcons

CHAPTER EIGHT
Working the Hill

"Nice game," Dad said, shaking Ben's hand as he reached the car.

"Best one yet," Ben said. "What's the hurry?"

"We're going to Larry's race."

"Oh yeah."

Larry was competing in an important cross-country race that afternoon. The meet was at a park just a few miles away.

Mom leaned over the back seat and handed Ben a small paper bag with a peanut butter sandwich, a container of yogurt, and an apple.

"Thanks," he said. "You don't even realize that you're hungry when you're running that hard. But as soon as you stop, you're like, 'I'm starving!'"

When they reached the park, Ben spotted Larry's team in their green sweatsuits jogging in a grassy field. The shirts said LINCOLN in big white letters. There were lots of other teams, too. Ben slammed the car door shut and ran over to his brother.

"Hey, Larry!" Ben shouted as he got closer.

Larry gave a quick wave, but he didn't smile and he kept jogging.

"We won," Ben said, running next to his brother.

"That's good." Larry was staring straight ahead and looked very serious.

The team members all stopped running and began to stretch. They bent their knees a little and reached for the ground.

"I *almost* scored," Ben said. "But I made some pretty good passes."

Larry shut his eyes and nodded. He stood straight up and reached his arms overhead. Then he jogged away again.

What's his problem? Ben thought. He didn't bother to follow Larry. He walked back across the field toward his parents.

"Larry totally ignored me," he said.

"He's concentrating," Mom said.

"This is a huge race for him," Dad said. "He's bound to be nervous."

Ben hadn't thought about that. "I guess he needs to focus," he said.

"He certainly does," Dad said. "You know how it is. When you're in a soccer game, you aren't thinking about anything but that, right? It can be even harder in a race."

Ben agreed. If you messed up in a race, you didn't have a teammate to help you out. When Ben had stumbled in the soccer game, Jordan had scored anyway. He could just imagine how it would be if things went wrong in a long race like this.

Larry would be running 3,000 meters, just a little less than two miles. And this park was hilly. They'd be following paths through the woods, up and down short, steep hills and longer, more gradual ones. And they'd be running fast. No wonder Larry was being quiet.

The runners were lining up at the start. Ben counted twelve teams on the line. Larry was usually the third- or fourth-fastest runner on his team, and the team was one of the best in the area.

"He's hoping to finish in the top ten overall," Dad said. "His team has a good chance to win the meet."

Ben followed his parents as they walked toward the woods.

"If you time it right, you can see nearly all of the race," Dad said. "Cross-country is one of the only sports where the spectators have to move around, too."

The whistle blew to start the race and the pack of runners streamed across the grassy field. Several runners sprinted to the front.

"They'll never keep up that pace," Dad said. "Larry's playing it smart."

Larry was near the front of the pack, but he looked calm and relaxed.

The runners circled around the grassy area and turned onto a dirt path that would lead them into the woods. After a few minutes, four runners had broken away from the others and opened a 20-meter lead. Larry's teammate Devin was among them.

Ben quickly counted the runners ahead of his brother. "He's in sixteenth," he said.

"That's good," Dad replied. "The hills will make a big difference. Every athlete has to work hard, but staying in control is the key. Larry is pacing himself just fine."

As the runners entered the woods, Ben's parents headed toward a different path. "They'll pass this point in a few minutes," Dad said. "Up this hill."

A large group of parents and others were at the side of the path atop the hill. Soon Ben could see Devin and one other runner climbing the other side.

"Go, Devin!" Ben's father called. "Relax and work this hill."

Two other runners followed closely behind, and then came five more tightly bunched, including another of Larry's Lincoln teammates.

"Where's Larry?" Ben asked as several seconds passed.

And then he saw him. He'd moved into twelfth, but a huge pack of runners was just behind him.

"Come on, Larry!" Mom called.

"Top ten is right here," Dad shouted, pointing toward the pack.

All of the runners were breathing hard and struggling as they climbed the steep hill. They were almost to the midway point of the race.

Ben watched in awe as the runners powered past him, their legs dotted with mud and their arms pumping hard.

After Larry passed, Ben and his parents moved quickly back to the field. The race course was two large laps, so the runners would be covering the same path again.

Ben made circles with his thumbs and first fingers, holding them up to his eyes like binoculars. He kept his focus on Larry, who was moving closer to the pack as they ran on flatter ground.

After Larry entered the woods, Ben turned and ran to the top of the hill again. It was only a minute or so before Devin appeared, with that same runner right on his shoulder.

The other runners had spread out a bit, coming up the hill alone or in pairs. The second runner from Larry's team was in sixth.

Every couple of seconds another runner came into view. And then there was Larry, in tenth.

"Yeah!" Ben shouted. "Looking great!"

But Larry's arms were close to his sides now and his mouth was twisted in pain.

"Don't think about it!" Ben shouted. "Just sprint up that hill!"

Larry seemed to relax his shoulders a bit. He leaned forward slightly and moved closer to the next runner.

"All that hard work," Ben said, shaking a fist at Larry. "Make it pay off."

Larry nodded to Ben as he ran past. As he reached the top of the hill, Larry began swinging his arms again. He opened up his stride as he moved downhill, and within a few seconds he had moved ahead of his opponent.

Ben hurried partway down the side of the hill so he could see the finish line. Larry

was in ninth place and he had about 200 meters left to run. The eighth-place runner was
a few yards ahead, and Larry was gaining on
him.

They both were sprinting now, but Larry
looked stronger. He surged ahead in the last
few meters and crossed the finish line in
eighth.

That took guts! Ben thought.

Ben ran across the field and joined Larry and his teammates. Larry had his hands on his knees and his legs were shaking a little, but he had a big smile, too. "Looks like we won it, knucklehead," he said, punching Ben lightly on the arm.

"You were awesome," Ben said. "That hill was a killer."

Ben looked at Devin, who had put his sweatsuit back on and was already jogging. "Did he win?" Ben asked.

"Yeah," Larry said. "We got first, sixth, and eighth, and I think we had two others in the top fifteen. No way any other team could beat that."

Ben was surprised how exciting the race had been. And how hard they'd run.

"Too bad soccer and cross-country are in the same season," he said. "That looked like fun."

Larry laughed. "I wouldn't exactly call it fun," he said. "There's nothing fun about sprinting up a hill when your legs have turned to butter. But yeah, I wouldn't trade it for anything."

CHAPTER NINE
Too Much Thinking

"This is a big test today," Ben said to Kim as they approached the field for their next game. "We haven't played two good games in a row yet."

"We will," Kim said. "We've improved a ton."

"That's what we thought a few weeks ago," Ben said, shaking his head. But he was feeling good about the Bobcats' chances. And he was very excited.

Ben waved to Jordan and Omar, who were already warming up on the field. He stopped to put on his shin guards.

"We just need to be smarter," Ben said. "I've made too many errors in too many games."

The Wolves were in last place in the Southern Division, but Ben knew that didn't mean much. The Falcons had been in last place when the Bobcats played them, but that game hadn't even been close. *I'm confident*, Ben thought, *but definitely not* over*confident*.

The day was dry and windy, and nearly all of the leaves had fallen from the trees. Ben kept his sweatshirt on while the Bobcats jogged and practiced shooting and passing.

Coach Patty clapped her hands and gathered the team around her. Ben rubbed his hands together; they were cold. Playing goalie would be hard today because that ball could sting. He noticed that Shayna was wearing gloves and figured she'd be the starting goalie.

Coach put Kim, Mark, and Omar on the front line and Erin and Darren on defense. Ben had started every game this season, but he knew that the coach played everyone about the same amount.

Then again, he'd cost his team a few wins this season. Maybe Coach thought they'd do better without him.

He stood on the sideline next to Jordan as the game began.

Jordan kept hopping up and down. "It's colder than I thought," he said.

"We'll be warm as soon as we get in the game," Ben said.

"Hope so."

Ben shoved his hands into the front pouch of his sweatshirt. "Go, Bobcats!" he yelled.

The Wolves had only one win this season, but they looked strong and fast as the game got under way. Twice in the first few minutes one of their players charged down the field with the ball, dodging past the Bobcats' defenders and taking a shot. Shayna stopped them both.

The second time, Shayna punted the ball and it landed right in front of Mark near midfield. He quickly passed to Erin, who took one step with it and sent it up the field to Omar.

"Good passing!" Jordan called. He turned to

Ben. "There's the difference," he said. "The Wolves play like we used to—everybody for himself. They've got good athletes, but they don't work together."

Ben remembered to add something about passing to the list of soccer tips he kept at home.

When Jordan took a few quick steps along the sideline to get closer to the action, Ben did, too. That moved him closer to Loop and Alex, who were waiting to play in the next game.

"Your team is looking good," Loop said.

"Thanks," Ben replied, keeping his eyes on the field.

"I guess that's because you aren't playing."

Ben glared at Loop. But Loop laughed. "Just kidding," he said. "Good luck today."

Mark had the ball near the corner, and he was guarded closely by a couple of the Wolves. But he managed to loft the ball out in front of the goal, and Kim fielded it cleanly.

She faked a shot, then slid the ball to Omar. He was wide open, and he booted it safely into the goal.

Ben jumped high and smacked hands with Jordan. But he couldn't help wondering why Kim could make such a great fake while he couldn't.

It was Omar's first goal of the season. He sprinted back to the Bobcats' side of the field and dropped to his knees with his arms up. Mark and the others slapped him on the back.

Coach Patty clapped her hands again. "Get right back to it!" she called. "Celebrate *after* the game."

She was right. The Wolves weren't ready to pack up just yet. They scored a goal less than a minute later. Shayna blocked a shot and it bounced back onto the field, and one of the Wolves scored off the rebound.

Coach turned to Ben and Jordan. "Get in there for Mark and Omar," she said. "Hustle."

Ben bumped fists with Omar as they changed places. "Great shot," he said.

The red-haired player who'd scored for the Wolves was directly across from Ben. He went to a different school, but Ben had seen him before. He was tall, like Mark, and he was probably the fastest runner on the field.

I'll keep an eye on him, Ben thought. *He's dangerous.*

And even though the Wolves didn't pass nearly as much as the Bobcats, their two best players kept the game very close. It was true that teamwork could help overcome a stronger group of players, but sometimes one or two standouts could keep a team in a game.

That proved to be the case during the rest of the first half. Ben, Jordan, and Kim worked well together, moving up the field several times and getting off a few shots. But the red-haired kid swooped in to take the ball away a few times, and his teammate with the ponytail made several long runs with the ball.

On defense, Erin stole the ball from the girl with the ponytail and kicked it hard toward midfield. Ben tried to chase it down, but it was too far away, and it rolled out of bounds.

Ben put his hands on his knees and took a few deep breaths while the red-haired kid ran after the ball. The cold air was making it harder to breathe.

"We've been running like mad," Ben said to Kim.

"Keep it up," she said. "Sooner or later we'll get a break."

But a throw-in brought the ball deep into the Bobcats' zone, and the blue- and brown-shirted players scrambled after it. Darren kicked it up the field, and Ben took control. The field was open ahead of him except for that ponytailed girl.

The grass was dry, so Ben knew he wouldn't slip if he tried that fake. Things were set up perfectly. His opponent was steady in her stance, waiting for Ben to approach. He took another quick step with the ball, then shifted toward the sideline.

The girl moved to block his path, and Ben brought his left foot over the ball. He stopped short, then tapped the ball away from the sideline with the outside of his foot. He charged up the field after it.

But he hadn't fooled her at all. Ben was off-balance as he tried to cut away, and the defender took control of the ball. She ran deep into the Bobcats' zone with it and made a quick fake that left Erin standing still. And then the girl fired the ball past Shayna and into the goal.

Ben shut his eyes and let out his breath hard. He'd almost made the fake, but somehow

the defender had seen it coming. He caught up to Jordan and shook his head. "It's like what you told me about Alex," he said. "I looked where I was going and gave away the fake."

"Don't worry about it," Jordan said with a tight smile. "It's still anybody's game. Keep working."

The Bobcats had fallen behind again, despite all that hard work and good passing. And Ben had made another misstep trying to do that fake.

They were trailing 2–1, and Ben knew that the second half would be an even tougher test than the first. And they couldn't afford another loss. Not if they wanted to stay in the race for the play-offs.

CHAPTER TEN
Power and Speed

Ben peeled an orange and sat on the bench between Erin and Jordan as they waited for the second half to begin. He didn't feel cold anymore. The sun had come out but the air was still cool. It wasn't the sun that had made him warm, though; it was all that running.

"That team is fast," he said.

"So are we," Jordan said. "This game will come down to who has more guts."

"Us!" Ben said.

"It *should* be us," Jordan replied. "Nobody works harder than we do."

Ben nodded. He thought back to the way Larry had run that cross-country race. He'd reached down deep and used every ounce of energy. Ben would do that, too.

Ben looked across the field to the other bench, where the Wolves were gathered around their coach. They had two very good athletes on that team. And they'd both scored goals in the first half.

Coach Patty announced the lineup for the second half: Omar as goalie; Mark, Erin, and Shayna on the front line; and Darren and Jordan on defense. She sent them onto the field.

"This will be your last rest," she said to Kim and Ben. "I'm hoping that we can tie the score before you go back in, or at least stay within one goal. You two work very well together, so

I'm confident that you can get us at least one more score."

Ben watched the action with his fists clenched, eager to get back on the field. The Wolves kept the ball for most of the first few minutes of the half, but they still weren't passing. They never got close enough for a shot.

"They're leaving this side of the field wide open," Kim said softly to Ben. "Let's take advantage of that when we get in there."

"Yeah," Ben said. He glanced over to his parents and Larry, who were standing near the sideline. Larry gave a slight wave and walked over.

"That red-haired kid is super fast," Larry said, "but he isn't very good at keeping the ball close to him. He kicks it and chases it. You should be able to take it away pretty easily."

But just as Larry said it, that player took the ball at midfield and darted past Mark and

Shayna. He angled across the field and outran Erin, too.

Now he was in a race with Darren for the ball. Darren got to it first, but all he could do was knock it out of bounds. The other kid picked it up and immediately tossed a long throw-in toward the Bobcats' goal.

"Grab it!" Ben shouted, hoping Omar could pick it up before anyone got to it. But the girl with the ponytail was between Omar and the ball. She fielded it with her foot and circled into the goal area.

Ben held his breath as the red-haired kid raced toward the goal. He was wide open, and a simple pass would have meant a goal for sure. But the girl was looking to shoot it herself, and Jordan easily stole the ball and booted it ahead to Mark.

"Great defense, Jordan!" Ben yelled. "Good hustle!"

The Bobcats had dodged a disaster. Both teams battled hard for several more minutes but neither could mount an attack. When the ball went out of bounds behind the Bobcats' goal, Coach Patty yelled, "Substitution!" to the referee.

She waved at Mark and Erin to come out, and she sent Kim and Ben to the front line. Shayna shifted back to play defense. Jordan joined Kim and Ben up front.

Ben grabbed Kim and Jordan by the elbows. "Speed," he said firmly. "Speed and passing. Just like we've been doing in practice."

Ben had a lot of confidence in these two teammates. He knew that Mark was the strongest player on the team, and that everyone played hard. But he and Kim and Jordan seemed to have a good sense of each other. They knew where to move to be in the best position for a pass.

Since Kim and Ben had taken a long rest, they were able to outrun their opponents at first. So the Bobcats kept control of the ball, managing a series of charges toward the goal and a couple of good shots. Kim's first shot flew just wide of the goal, and Jordan's was tipped aside at the last second by the goalie.

"Keep up the pressure," Ben said. "We've got them on their heels."

But the Wolves held their one-goal lead as the minutes ticked away. Ben took a pass from Kim near the sideline and looked around the field. Kim was covered closely and Jordan was too far away. So Ben waved his hand toward Shayna, who was hanging back on defense.

Ben dribbled to the center of the field, then kicked the ball backward to Shayna. "We need support," he said. "Stay up with us."

Shayna passed to Jordan, and Jordan passed it right back. Shayna then passed to Ben, and

she kept moving forward as Ben and Jordan sent passes back to her. Slowly the Bobcats were getting closer to the Wolves' goal.

Ben could tell that the Wolves were getting tired. The Bobcats' swift passing was keeping them moving, but they weren't getting close to the ball.

The next time Ben got it, he faked a pass to

Shayna and dribbled as fast as he could along the sideline. He could see his three teammates moving toward the goal as the defenders came out to stop him.

He was nearly to the corner and the defenders were closing in. Just before they reached him, he sent a hard pass across the field, zinging over the top of the grass. Ben fell forward and landed with his hands spread out. He rolled to his side and crawled back up. He heard lots of shouting.

What happened? he wondered. Kim and Jordan and Shayna were leaping in front of the goal, and the Wolves goalie was staring into the net. He was staring at the ball!

Ben raced to the cluster of Bobcats. "Who scored?" he asked, smacking hands with Jordan.

"Kim did," Jordan said. "Perfect pass!"

"Couldn't have been better," Kim said. "I

didn't even break stride. The ball was right where I wanted it. The goalie never had a chance."

"How much time?" Ben asked the referee as they ran back to midfield.

The referee glanced at his watch. "About three minutes," he said.

"That's plenty," Ben said. "Let's get the ball back."

With the score tied, both teams began to play even harder. The difference was that the Wolves kicked the ball hard and chased after it, while the Bobcats made accurate passes to each other. Ben knew that his team's strategy *should* work better, but the Wolves had power and speed.

Darren made a nice steal near the Bobcats' goal, and he fed Ben a pass. The field was open in front of him.

Just like before, Ben sprinted along the

sideline with the ball, moving into the Wolves' side of the field. A pair of defenders closed in on him, so he pivoted quickly and sent the ball back to Kim, who was trailing behind.

The defenders chased after Kim, giving Ben a perfect chance to move to an open area near the goal. Kim passed ahead to Jordan, and Jordan made a crisp lead pass to Ben.

Ben trapped the ball and turned toward the goal, moving up the field. Just one player blocked his path. Ben picked up his pace, dribbling the ball at full speed.

As the Wolves defender angled toward him, Ben stepped over the ball, dodging to his left. The defender went for the fake. Ben swept the ball to the right with the outside of his foot, and now the space between him and the goal was wide open.

After three more steps Ben found himself in front of the goalie. It was a tough angle to

shoot from, but Ben shot the ball hard and the goalie left his feet, diving toward it. The ball rose past the goalie's hands and sank deep into the net.

The Bobcats had the lead!

Ben circled around the goal and raced back onto the field, leaping into the air as he reached Kim. He shook his fist and opened his mouth wide. He couldn't yell; his throat was too tight with emotion. He hadn't even thought about those moves this time. They just happened.

"Great passing!" he finally said.

"Great shooting!" Kim replied.

The last couple of minutes were a blur for Ben as he and his teammates kept the pressure on. The Wolves never even crossed midfield. The Bobcats had won another game.

As Ben ran off the field, Loop was running on. Loop held up his hand and Ben slapped it with a high five.

"Great game," Loop said.

"For once, we agree," Ben replied, beaming.

Ben looked around at his smiling team-mates. They'd finally won two straight. Over their last five games, they were 3-1-1, as good as any team in the league. Things were definitely looking up for the Bobcats.

They'd made it happen today. They'd played harder than they ever had, and they'd played smart.

Best of all for Ben, he'd finally made that fake in a game.

Larry was right—everybody has bad days and great days. *The great days make you forget about the bad ones in a hurry*, Ben thought. *We can beat any team in this league.*

He couldn't wait to prove that at next week's game.

BEN'S TOP TIPS FOR SOCCER PLAYERS

• Practice shooting and passing the ball with the inside of your foot instead of your toes. You'll be more accurate.

• Keep your eye on the ball when you pass it or shoot it.

• If you usually kick the ball with your right foot, try using your left. You'll be harder to stop if you can use both feet.

• Sometimes the most effective pass will go backward. Find an open teammate to pass to, then move to an open spot for a return pass.

• When playing defense, watch your opponent from the waist up instead of looking at the ball. That will tell you which direction he plans to dribble and keep you from getting faked out.

Don't miss
Kickers #3: *Benched*

It's a race to the Kickers soccer league play-offs. Nine-year-old Ben is pretty sure that if the Bobcats win two of their last three games, they'll earn a tournament spot. But in their game against the Tigers, the Bobcats are a mess on the field—they're not passing well at all—and Ben decides to take control. Someone has to win this thing, and his teammates just aren't measuring up.

Then the whistle blasts, the red card waves, and Ben is out—benched for dangerous moves. Not only that, he's barred from the next game, too—a key bout against the Rabbits. How can he possibly help his team to the play-offs from the *sidelines*?

The Kickers series, from award-winning sports novelist Rich Wallace, features nonstop soccer action, black-and-white art, and league statistics and soccer tips throughout.

Also available:
Kickers #1: *The Ball Hogs*
Kickers #4: *Game-Day Jitters*